New Neighbors

by **Lisa Norby**   illustrated by **Mike Tofanelli**

Table of Contents

CHAPTER 1
New Town

Jeremy sat in front of his computer. His friend Anthony wasn't online this afternoon. He wondered what Anthony was doing. Maybe he was shooting baskets with the O'Neill twins. They had a hoop and backboard set up in their driveway. On a summer afternoon there would usually be a few kids there, practicing their shots.

Anthony might even be swimming in the Baileys' pool. At the end of summer the Bailey girls usually had pool parties. All the neighborhood kids were invited over for an afternoon swim and a barbecue with hamburgers and hot dogs.

Jeremy sighed. He sat down at the computer and wrote an e-mail to Anthony:

"You should see our new house! It's double the size of the old one. The kitchen appliances are all stainless steel. We have a gigantic freezer, big enough to stock enough food for two winters! So far, we haven't used the appliances much. Mom and Dad haven't had much time to cook. Since Dad's new office is downtown, it's a long commute for him. He usually doesn't get home until after eight.

"We also have a big backyard. Dad says he can't wait until I'm a few years older. Taking care of it will be my job. But my plan is to convince Dad that building a swimming pool out there would be a great idea. Wouldn't it be awesome to have an Olympic-sized pool? I could swim and perfect my diving skills. Mom and Dad could get exercise. And I'd be the most popular kid in the neighborhood. Also, there would be a lot less lawn to mow. LOL."

LOL means "laugh out loud." But Jeremy wasn't laughing. There was no way he was going to be the most popular kid in the neighborhood. That was just a fantasy. But he didn't want to tell Anthony the truth.

It had been two weeks since his family had moved to Gatesburg. In all that time, Jeremy hadn't met a single kid his own age. In fact, he hadn't met any kids at all.

In his old neighborhood, there was always something going on. After school, children brought out their roller skates and bicycles. They played one-on-one at the O'Neills' house. They skateboarded in the school playground.

Jeremy hadn't realized that Gatesburg would be so different. It was a brand new suburb and the houses were bigger and farther apart. Some were still under construction. Even the finished homes appeared empty because trees, grass, and flowers hadn't been planted yet. He rarely saw the owners outside. There was hardly any traffic on the streets. And there were no sidewalks either.

Jeremy could usually talk to his parents about things that worried him, but lately they hadn't had time to listen. They were preoccupied with getting the house in order. They were busy with chores or dashing out on various errands.

Jeremy's mother, a financial consultant, had her office at the back of the house. This morning, Jeremy had helped her unpack her office equipment. But by the afternoon he was bored and tired of being indoors. He decided to explore the neighborhood.

CHAPTER 2
Matthew

Two blocks from his own street, Jeremy heard a welcome sound. Someone was dribbling a basketball on a concrete driveway!

The basketball player appeared to be about Jeremy's age. Jeremy approached, trying to act casual. "What's up?" he asked.

The boy turned around. He gave Jeremy a friendly smile. "Hi, I'm Matthew, but you can call me Matt," he said. "Want to shoot baskets?"

His speech was careful, as if he had to think about every word.

Jeremy could see that Matt was a good basketball player. But there was something different about him. Jeremy felt awkward and stood there not knowing what to say.

But Matt didn't seem offended. "Okay," he said. "Then I'll shoot."

Matt shot underhanded.

"Missed," said Matt.

Matt retrieved the ball and tried again. This time, he made a basket.

He turned back to Jeremy. "Now you," he said.

Jeremy shrugged and then he caught the ball that Matt bounced in his direction. With a graceful one-handed move, he flipped the ball in the direction of the basket. It hit the backboard and bounced to one side.

"Missed!" called Matt.

Jeremy stepped up to the imaginary free throw line. This time, he took careful aim.

The ball swished through the hoop.

"Let's go best out of ten," Jeremy suggested.

Matt got his first five shots in. Jeremy thought he was surely going to lose, but the final score was seven baskets for Jeremy, six for Matt.

"You're pretty good," Jeremy said.

"I am good. I was in the Olympics."

"Right," Jeremy said. But he didn't believe it.

Jeremy hung around for a few more minutes before he said goodbye to Matt and started for home. Matt seemed like a nice kid, even if he was a little different. But obviously he was stranger than he'd seemed at first. He was convinced he'd been in the Olympics!

That night Jeremy sent an e-mail to Anthony: "There's good news and bad news. The good news is that I met a kid two blocks away. He has his own basketball hoop in his driveway."

"What's the bad news?" Anthony e-mailed back.

"He's a little strange. He says he competed in the Olympics."

Later Anthony responded, "So what? He has a hoop."

Anthony was right. Jeremy went back to Matt's the next afternoon. In fact, he dropped by for the next three consecutive afternoons. He and Matt didn't talk much, and that was all right with Jeremy. He preferred shooting baskets to talking.

But Jeremy did find out a few things. Matt's family had moved to Gatesburg a year ago. Matt was a Pacers fan. Now he was far away from Indiana. "No more Pacers," Matt said sadly.

This was something new for Jeremy to worry about. He hadn't thought about his favorite sports teams. Would he remain loyal to his old teams or would he switch to local teams? He wanted to root for the same teams as the other kids, but it would be hard to change. Moving was extremely complicated.

CHAPTER 3
Worries

Finally, the subject of school came up. "My teacher will be Mrs. Fernandez," Jeremy said.

Matt grinned. "My teacher is Mrs. Fernandez too."

That surprised Jeremy. "We're in the same class?" he asked.

Matt seemed to be reciting something he had memorized. "Special ed is with Mrs. Marino after lunch and regular class is in the morning."

"Oh, I get it," said Jeremy. There had been a special education class at his old school. He'd never really known how to talk to those kids. He was afraid he would say the wrong thing and hurt their feelings so he just didn't talk to them at all.

"Good," he said. "We will be in the same class for part of the day."

But was it good? More than anything, Jeremy wanted to be popular at his new school. Classes started next week and he and Matt would be catching the bus at the same stop. Right away, the other kids would see him and Matt together. What would they think? Would they think he was another special education student? Would they want to be his friend?

Jeremy really liked Matt. Thinking about these things didn't make Jeremy feel good. Still, he did think about them.

He couldn't talk about his worries with his parents. He knew what they would say: "Do the right thing. Don't worry about what the other kids think."

He tried explaining his fears to Anthony. But his old friend didn't take him seriously. "We liked you back here," Anthony said in an e-mail. "I can't believe kids in Gatesburg would be much different."

Anthony was probably right. He was making a big deal out of nothing. Still, he stayed away from Matt's house on Wednesday. He didn't go over there on Thursday or Friday either.

On Saturday morning, Jeremy had chores to do. His mother had been going through the boxes and she was finding a lot of things that should have been thrown away before they moved. "I can't believe we brought this leaky garden hose with us," she said. "And we don't need this rusty screwdriver or these pliers either. We've just moved in, and the garage is already full of junk."

There was a trash pickup that afternoon so Jeremy carried the things his mom wanted thrown away down to the end of the driveway. He was on his last trip when he spied Matt walking up the street. At the same moment, he noticed his neighbors' German shepherd racing across their lawn. The dog's bark sounded fierce.

"Hey, Matt," he called out. "Look out to your right."

Matt heard his shouts. He flashed a big smile and waved. He didn't seem aware of the dog. Jeremy felt afraid for him. He dropped his armful of trash and ran down the road.

CHAPTER 4

Next-Door Neighbors

But the dog got to Matt first. Instead of attacking, he jumped up and licked Matt's face. Matt beamed. "Tiger is my friend," he said.

"Yeah." Jeremy was embarrassed that he had been afraid of the dog. Suddenly, it looked very friendly.

Another boy about Jeremy's age had followed the dog across the lawn. "Hey, Matt," he said. "How are you doing?"

The boy introduced himself as Ricky Alexander. He explained that he'd just gotten back from camp. That's why Jeremy hadn't seen him around. "But I see you've already met Matt," he said.

"I guess so," Jeremy agreed.

"Matt is our neighborhood celebrity. His basketball team won a medal in the state Special Olympics," Ricky explained.

"That's fantastic!" said Jeremy.

"I told you about it," Matt chimed in.

"That's right, Matt. You did tell me. I just didn't understand what you meant. Congratulations."

Jeremy had heard of the Special Olympics, but he didn't know much about it. That evening, he looked it up on the Internet. He found out that the games are international. Almost two million athletes with disabilities from around the world participate in them.

It was true that Matt was a local celebrity. Jeremy found three newspaper articles about his basketball team. One told how the team had won a medal at the state games. The other two showed them at a basketball clinic run by the state university.

Monday morning came and with it the first day of school. It wasn't easy. Jeremy had to get used to new classes, a new teacher, and new friends. Still, it wasn't as bad as he had anticipated. He already knew two kids on the school bus, Matt and Ricky.

Everyone in Mrs. Fernandez's class liked Matt. He worked hard, and he was always ready to try new things. Jeremy couldn't believe that he had been worried about being Matt's friend.

Ricky was a grade ahead of Matt and Jeremy. He was president of the school's computer club, and he soon invited Jeremy to join.

In November, the PTA held a fair to raise money for after-school programs. Ricky's dad was one of the organizers. Jeremy and some other computer club members set up a booth. They demonstrated programs for the grownups and answered their questions.

Matt made the biggest contribution to the fair. He got some basketball players from the university's team to show up. The players gave a basketball clinic in the gym. Jeremy even got his picture taken with them.

Jeremy e-mailed the picture to Anthony. "I still miss all you guys, but I am meeting interesting people here. Gatesburg is not as bad as I had thought."

Comprehension Check

Summarize

Use a Theme Map to record clues about the main message or idea of the story. Then use the map to summarize the story.

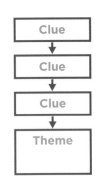

Think and Compare

1. Reread page 13. What is the theme of this page? What main idea is the author presenting here? *(Analyze Theme)*

2. Matt seems to know his strengths and his limitations. What are you skilled at? What skills would you like to improve? *(Apply)*

3. Why do you think Special Olympic games are so important? *(Evaluate)*